Badger's Bad Mood

Arthur A. Levine Books hardcover edition
published by Arthur A. Levine Books, an imprint
of Scholastic Press, May 1998

ISBN 0-590-21693-7

12 11 10 9 8 7 6 5 4 3 2 1   2 3 4 5 6 7/0

Printed in the U.S.A   08

First Scholastic paperback printing, December 2002

Badger's Bad Mood

HIAWYN ORAM ◆ SUSAN VARLEY

SCHOLASTIC INC.
New York Toronto London Auckland Sydney
Mexico City New Delhi Hong Kong Buenos Aires

Bat had been to deliver Badger's mail and now he brought news: Badger was in a bad mood.

"But Badger's *never* in a bad mood," said Fieldmouse.

"He is now," said Bat. "He just sits there, staring. Speak to him—he almost snaps your head off."

"I'll go and see him," said Mole.

"I'll go with you," said Squirrel.

So Mole, Squirrel, and Rabbit went to see Badger.

He was sitting in his chair, in the gloom, his face like a dark cloud.

"Now, now, Badger," fussed Squirrel. "This won't do at all."

She switched on a light.

"Turn that off!" snapped Badger. "And leave me be."

Squirrel and Rabbit were most offended. They scurried away, tutting to themselves.

Mole hung around in the shadows. He felt very sad. Without
Badger in a good mood *everything* seemed wrong. He rattled
some cups, cleared his throat, and opened and closed a cupboard.

"You still there, Mole?"

"Yes, yes. I'm still here!"

Badger heaved around in his chair. "I'm sorry about this. 'Spect
I'll get over it. But right now, I'm just no good, you know. *No
good for anything*."

"Don't worry," said Mole worriedly. "We'll just wait."

But waiting for Badger to get over his bad mood wasn't that easy. The animals were very impatient.

"He was going to help me choose a holiday," said Bat, waving his holiday brochures.

"Perhaps we should get him some ginger ale," said Rabbit.

"And some puzzles to take his mind off things," said Squirrel.

"Well, take him something," said Rat. "We're supposed to be going fishing today!"

"I've a doctor friend staying," said Stoat. "I'll take her over. She'll fix him up."

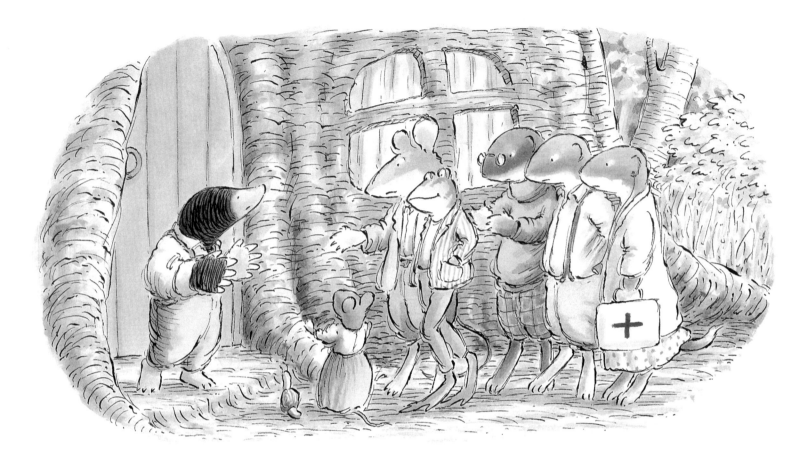

Badger, however, was having none of it.

"Close the curtains," he begged Mole. "Keep them away."

Mole stood guard at the door. "I'm sorry, but he's not seeing anyone."

"Well, we can't wait forever," said Frog. "Make him see reason, Molie."

"Snap him out of it," said Weasel.

"I'll see what I can do," said Mole.

When they had all gone away, Mole watched Badger staring and dozing and turning heavily in his chair.

He remembered his words. *No good for anything.*

Then he crept over to Badger's desk and very quietly borrowed some paper and pens and pencils.

The next morning a poster appeared, pinned to a tree in the clearing.

AWARDS CEREMONY

Tomorrow night in this clearing
awards will be presented
for everything.
Presenter:
Stoat's Friend the Doctor
Master of Ceremonies:
MOLE

Afterwards there'll be
juice and cakes,
music and dancing.

Dress:
Your best.

Everyone got excited.

"I'm bound to win the Fairy Cake Award," said Squirrel.

"Maybe I'll win the Slow Dancing," said Miss Snail.

They spent the rest of the day wondering who was going to win what for what and working on what they were going to wear.

Meanwhile, Mole went to see Badger.

"You'll have to come, of course. A little bird tells me you may be getting something."

Badger's eyes moved sharply for the first time in days.

"Really?" His voice had some edge to it. Some color.

"S'pose my tuxedo needs a press. You wouldn't help me with that, would you, Mole?"

Mole helped Badger press his suit and waistcoat.

Then he ran home to press his own—not to mention prepare some speeches, write out certificates, order the juice and cakes, book the musicians, and set up the clearing!

"Whose idea was this anyway?" he kept saying to himself. "I'll never be ready!"

But somehow, by the time everyone started arriving for the ceremony, he was ready.

He showed Stoat's doctor friend to the platform.

Then, out of the corner of his eye, he saw Badger slipping in at the back. "Well, that's a relief," he sighed.

"Excuse me?" said the doctor.

"Nothing," said Mole. "Let's begin."

The first award did go to Squirrel for Fairy Cakes and
Miss Snail did win for Slow Dancing.
Frog won for Best Hopping and Most Gallant Courting.

Stoat won for Swimming, Weasel for Wiliness, Fieldmouse for Scurrying, Hedgehog for Eating The Most Potato Chips At One Sitting, Rat for Reading, Rabbit for First Aid, and Bat for Most Musical Accordion Playing.

"And now," announced Mole. "We come to the last section." He cleared his throat. "The award for Always Knowing The Best Way Through the Woods . . . goes to . . ." There was an expectant hush.

"Badger!"

The clapping and cheering was deafening.

When it had died down, Mole cleared his throat again.

"And to save yourself a trip back to your seat . . . the award for Always Knowing What To Do In A Crisis . . . *Badger!* "

Mole waited for the applause to fade.

"And . . . the award for Always Being There For Others . . . *Badger!* The award for Most Needed And Depended On . . . *Badger!* And finally . . . the award for Most Loved Whatever His Mood . . . *BADGER!* "

The crowd rose, clapping and calling, "Bravo!"

Badger blushed and bowed and bowed and blushed and fumbled with all his certificates.

"Oh my, oh my," he whispered to Mole. "This is too much!"

"No more than you deserve," said Mole.

"Tell me," said Badger as he and Mole took a moment together after the ceremony, "whose idea was all this?"

Mole blinked slowly. "Um . . . uh . . . I . . ."

"Well," said Badger, "whoever it was deserves a medal. Two medals. Because, y'know, now and again, everyone needs to hear . . ."

"How much they're loved?" said Mole.

"And *appreciated*," bowed Badger.

"You said it," sighed Mole giving Badger a hug. Then he stepped onto the dance floor and made his happiest announcement yet . . .

"*OK everyone, Badger's back! Let's DANCE!*"

About the Author

HIAWYN ORAM is the author of over thirty books published around the world. Her awards have included the Japanese Picture Book Award for *Angry Arthur*, and the French Prix du Livre Culturel for *Just Like Us*. In addition to being an author of books for children, she writes for the theater and television, and is the mother of two sons, Maximilian and Felix.

About the Illustrator

SUSAN VARLEY has also received international recognition for her work. Her first book, *Badger's Parting Gifts*, won the prestigious Mother Goose Award in England, as well as the French Prix de la Fondation and the German Wilhelm-Hauff Award. *Booklist* said, "The mood and style of Varley's line work is akin to that of E.H. Shephard, while a full palette of delicate watercolor hues adds appeal and warmth."

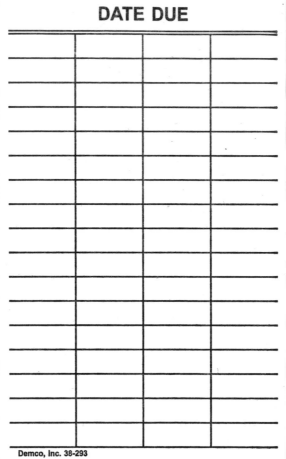

DATE DUE